followers

adam fleming petty

This publication is made possible by the funding provided by the Shaheen College of Arts and Sciences and the English Department at the University of Indianapolis. Special thanks to IngramSpark and to those students who judged, edited, designed, and published this chapbook: Rachel Holtzclaw, Adam Kuhn, and Rachael Neawedde.

The poem that opens this novella is attributed to Mary Stevenson.

UNIVERSITY *of*
INDIANAPOLIS.

Published by Etchings Press
1400 E. Hanna Ave.
Indianapolis, IN 46227
All rights reserved

etchings.uindy.edu
www.uindy.edu/cas/english

Printed by IngramSpark
ingramspark.com

Published in the United States of America

978-0-9903475-4-5

23 22 21 20 19 18 17 16   2 3 4 5
Second edition, 2019

One night I dreamed a dream.

I was walking along the beach with the LORD.

Across the dark sky flashed scenes from my life.

In each scene, I noticed two sets of footprints in the sand, one belonging to me, the other belonging to the LORD.

Sometimes, however, there was only one set of footprints.

This bothered me because it was during the low periods of my life, when I was suffering from anguish, sorrow or defeat, that I could see only one set of footprints.

I asked the LORD about my problem.

I said, "You promised me, LORD, that if I followed you, you would walk with me always. But I have noticed that during the most trying periods of my life, there was only one set of footprints in the sand. Why, when I needed you most, were you not there for me?"

The LORD replied, "My precious child, the years when you saw only one set of footprints,

it was then that I carried you."

1

I arrived at the airport an hour before her flight was scheduled to arrive. Since I had the time, I ducked into the bathroom to see how I looked. I spent all morning getting dressed, and I wanted to make sure I looked just right.

I was wearing a gray V-neck sweater over a button-down shirt, white with thin blue stripes, dark jeans, and a pair of anklet boots I was wearing for the first time. I had ordered them online after convincing Nancy they were more than just a splurge—I could use them for work—but now I wished I had worn something more familiar, my flats or even my Chucks. I lost my confidence for a moment. I gained it right back, however, when I looked up from my boots to the bathroom mirror and saw, once again, my scarf.

I looked so good. It was prideful to say that, but it was true. It was paisley, all blues and purples. It made me look so sophisticated, like I belonged in a coffee shop in New York or San Francisco. But what really made me look good was the fact that I didn't look like I was trying too hard. The scarf was meant for me. I was the girl the designers had in mind when they made it.

I left the bathroom and checked the arrivals. Carolina's flight had just landed. I walked to the baggage claim and stood before the carousel, waiting.

Carolina Colvin Diaz worked for Browsr, the biggest news site on the internet. Everyone shared its articles on Facebook, the lists of cats and laughing babies as well as the more serious human interest stories about prejudice and overcoming the trauma of sexual abuse. She was here to do a feature on Karen Wallin Kerry, my boss. It was going to be more than a story, in fact. She was going to make arrangements for Karen to get the help she needed. As Karen made progress, Carolina would follow along, writing a story that would raise awareness of an oft-misunderstood issue.

I had done my homework, reading her work on Browsr as well as her posts on social media. She was funny online, making jokes about shopping and how she couldn't stop eating glazed dough-nuts. I felt like I already knew her, which made it surprising when she stepped out of the gate and I didn't even recognize her until she was standing right in front of me, saying my name.

"Hannah Gustafson?"

That's me. Always waiting for someone else to introduce me.

It took me a second to respond. I was busy registering her outfit: jeans, pink t-shirt, and a cropped blazer with the sleeves rolled up. Casual and sophisticated at once.

"Yes, hi! Sorry I missed you. My mind must have been wan-dering. How was your flight?"

"Flights, plural. Took me three connections to get here. Last one was this tiny plane that only sat about twelve people. Felt like a minivan with wings."

"It does take some work getting here, but it's worth it! Colo-rado's so beautiful. The mountains and the fields really speak of God's glory."

"It's my first time out West."

"You'll have to go hiking!"

I was coming on too strong. I needed to focus on the present before I could plan for the future.

"I was just waiting for your luggage. I'll help you with it."

"This is all I brought." She indicated a gym bag slung over her shoulder, a laptop bag, and a purse. "Saves the hassle of having to check anything."

"That's so smart! Here, let me take something."

"Thanks, but I got it."

"I insist!"

I did. I took the gym bag from her shoulder, making an awk-ward dance of it. But I recovered quickly and led her out to the car.

Whenever I picked up guests from the airport, I always liked to keep silent for the first few minutes of the drive. It let them take in the majesty of the scenery, the rivers flowing down mountainsides, the open meadows where elk and foxes roamed. Once guests were acclimated, I deployed my sole talent: making small talk. I can go on for hours and hours, keeping things pleasant while not saying much of anything. It comes in handy in my job as Karen's personal assistant, keeping people occupied as they wait to talk to the person who's really important.

"Karen's looking forward to hearing what you have to say."

"I look forward to hearing what she has to say."

"She can't wait to see what you have in mind. Browsr! This will give Karen a whole new audience. We don't interact with secular media that often, but the timing for this couldn't be better."

It's helpful to go into detail when talking with non-believers, I've found. You want to make sure they understand.

"Secular?" said Carolina.

"I'm sorry, are you a believer? I shouldn't make assumptions like that. The faithful work in secular industries all the time. Somebody has to witness to them!"

"I'm not a believer. I'm just here to do my job. I can do that even if I don't believe, right?"

"Yes, of course! I apologize. I just keep assuming, don't I?"

This wasn't going well. I needed to get her talking about herself.

"You work for Browsr, so you live in New York?"

"The offices are in Manhattan, but I live in Brooklyn like everyone else. Fort Greene, to be specific."

"I've been there a few times. Karen has spoken at churches and conferences there. They were work trips, so I didn't get to see much of the city. I did go to Times Square, though."

"You didn't get groped by Spider-Man, did you?"

I thought she was telling me something personal. I was ready to pull into the nearest parking lot and have her tell me all about it, but she said it was nothing, just a bad joke. I tried to keep the conversation moving.

"How long have you worked there?"

"Almost a year. My first job out of college. I know I'm lucky to get it. Plenty of my friends are just spinning their wheels working as baristas, but I haven't really made my mark yet. I just make listicles."

"I love those! Which ones were yours?"

"My biggest hit is '17 Virgenes de Guadalupe Who Can't Even.' Pictures of Virgen statues with funny or weird facial expressions."

"I didn't see that one."

I had seen it, actually. It was part of my research. But I wanted to keep her talking.

"It helped me get this assignment, actually. My editor said I had a good feel for religious content."

"Oh, Virgen. Like the Virgin Mary?"

"Yes, sorry, I should have mentioned that."

"Wait, does that mean you're Catholic? I thought you said you weren't a believer." I was excited, and tried not to overreact. I don't think it worked.

"Catholics can't be believers?"

"Of course they can! I just don't know very much about them. Takes all kinds, right? Demonstrates more of God's glory."

"Or gives us something to fight about," said Carolina.

"That too, I suppose. So are you?"

"Am I what?"

"Catholic?"

Carolina paused for several moments, making me worry that my question had offended her. Finally, she said, "I think so."

Such a calm answer was generous on her part, and I didn't want to press any further. I would have been happy to spend the rest of the drive making harmless remarks about the scenery, but she had a question for me.

"What are evangelicals?"

I wished she had asked me anything else. I never understood these matters of doctrine and denominations. Steve was the one who knew about all that. Karen didn't even talk about theology, really, although I wasn't sure if that was because she didn't understand, or she didn't think it was important. She told God's story by telling her story, was how she put it. At least she used to.

But Carolina was interested in what I had to say. I liked having her attention, and I didn't want to lose it.

"Evangelicals think, or they believe, I guess, that the most important thing in life is your personal relationship with Jesus. No one else comes between that, not a priest, or a saint, or anything like that. It's just you and the Lord."

"So you don't have any priests?"

"We have pastors, of course. They're the leaders of the church, but they're not leaders like priests are."

"Not like priests how?"

"I . . . I don't know, honestly. I didn't go to college, I didn't study any of this stuff. You can ask Steve when we get to the house. He's Karen's soulguard."

"Her what?"

"Like a bodyguard, but for her soul."

"Is that a real position, like a pastor?"

"No, that's just what he calls himself."

Was she interviewing me? Were my words on record? Maybe I should have been more careful in the questions I was asking her. I was representing Karen, after all. But I couldn't stop talking. Perhaps she sensed that, because she began asking questions I wasn't supposed to answer.

"I don't think I understand everything that's going on," she said. "That means I need to ask questions in order to do my job. Can you answer them?"

"I'll try." I wanted so badly to tell her what she needed to know.

"My editor only gave me so much information about this assignment. Maybe that's all she knew, and she wants me to fill in the blanks. But here's what I do know: a few months ago, Karen stopped making public appearances. No conferences, no speeches. This was very sudden. There have been rumors going through the evangelical community, but nothing certain. My editor heard about this from her family—she grew up evangelical—and decided to look into it. She contacted Karen's people, and they said they'd be glad to have someone from Browsr come and visit. So here I am."

"Here you are! We can't wait to see how you're going to help."

"Help with what?"

She really didn't know? Her editor hadn't put the pieces together? Or hadn't Nancy told her? If that was the case, then did Nancy want to be the one to tell her?

I wanted to give Carolina the information she wanted, but I didn't know if I was supposed to. So what did I do? What else could I have done?

"Karen has a demon," I said.

2

Karen Wallin Kerry was the youngest of four children, but even before she could walk, the rest of her family looked up to her. She had that something special, that glow about her, and you just knew that God had special things planned for her.

Her teachers loved her, but so did her classmates, which was very rare. Everyone wanted to be her friend. She started singing solos in church when she was a little girl, and the whole congregation was struck by her poise, her self-composure, which would have been remarkable in an adult, to say nothing of a child. And on top of her poise, she had the voice of an angel.

Karen was friends with everyone, but there was one person she was especially close to: Nancy Gustafson, my mother. They met in junior high. Karen found Nancy in the girls' bathroom one day, crying. Some of the older girls were mean to her. Once Karen befriended her, however, she was spared from the cruelties of school, and Nancy stayed by her side, grateful.

Karen was active in church youth group throughout high school, leading outreach missions, giving her testimony on Wednesday nights. She made being a Christian seem not only cool, but brave. There were plenty of kids who came to Christ though her witness, and youth pastors from different churches in the area, even in different states, invited her to come and speak to their flocks. She was a featured speaker at several conferences during the summers, and when she invited people to come forward and dedicate their lives to Christ, she drew more people than anyone else.

In her senior year of high school, Karen went to a party at her friend Nancy's house. Nancy's family had a pool, and it was always open to Karen and her friends. Things were going great for Karen: she was headed for college in the fall, one of the best Christian schools in the country, where she was planning to double major in art and English. She had always been talented and creative, and she hoped to hone her gifts so she could use them to bring glory to God.

At the party, Karen decided to do something brave. There was a diving board at the pool, and she had always been hesitant to try it. She couldn't even say why, it was just a fear of hers. That night, however, she decided to place her trust in God and face her fear.

She stepped onto the diving board and walked out to the edge of it. All of her friends were there, encouraging her to go for it.

She didn't remember what happened next. Nancy did, though. Karen had begun to jump off the diving board, bouncing on her right leg to get some momentum, but her foot had slipped out from under her. She fell and hit her head on the edge of the board, then crashed into the water, unconscious.

Nancy had wanted to dive in and help her friend, but she couldn't move. Thankfully, Karen's father was there, and he dove in and pulled Karen out, surely saving his daughter from drowning. But there were still consequences.

Karen was paralyzed from the neck down. Her doctors said she would never recover, and would have to live in a wheelchair for the rest of her life.

Her family and friends were devastated. They met at Nancy's family's house to pray for a miracle. They did it around the clock. Every hour of the day, there was someone praying, pleading with God to prove the doctors wrong and heal Karen, give her a full recovery. Karen's father even walked out on the diving board, stood on its edge, and asked God to push him off the diving board and paralyze him in exchange for healing his daughter's body.

Karen, however, told everyone not to worry. If this was God's will, then she would accept it, gladly. The prayer meetings at Nancy's house began to taper off, until the only person left was Nancy. One night, she was sitting on the edge of the diving board, her bare feet skimming the water. Nancy opened her heart to God, letting him have his will in the matter. At that very moment, lying in her hospital bed, Karen felt a twinge in the big toe of her right foot.

Soon, all the feeling returned to her foot. But only her foot. The rest of her body remained paralyzed. If you had asked, her friends and family would have said this wasn't what they had in mind when they were praying to God. But to Karen, it was all the miracle she needed.

She learned how to do almost anything with her foot. She gripped a paintbrush between her toes and painted watercolors, Nancy adjusting the canvas as needed. She learned to type on a word processor and wrote down her thoughts in journal entries, poems, stories. Nancy organized her paintings and collected her writings, and before too long, there was more than enough to show. There were exhibitions of her paintings, volumes of her writings. Her paintings sold out; her books went to the top of the Christian bestseller list. As her health stabilized, she began traveling to the same churches and conferences where she had spoken before, only now the crowds she drew were much, much bigger. She even met and fell in love with a good Christian man, a worship leader named Mitch Kerry. She said no one could have asked God for so many blessings in one's life.

Life continued this way for years. Then one day, a few months ago, she felt something in her foot. Something that didn't feel right.

The house was in a valley out at the foot of the mountains, ridged on the sides and flat on the bottom, like a bowl. This was why we had bought the property. The whole house needed to be wheelchair-accessible, which meant no stairs. Karen wanted to be able to get into every room. Five bedrooms, three-and-a-half baths, and she could enter all of them.

We pulled into the driveway. I went to the trunk and took out Carolina's gym bag, slinging it over my shoulder in one swift motion. However, I did it so fast that the strap got caught on my scarf and just about choked me.

"You okay?" she asked.

"Fine, just a little clumsy."

She helped set the strap square on my shoulder, then readjusted my scarf for me.

"It's cute," she said.

If embarrassing myself was what it took for her to notice my scarf, it was worth it.

At the front door, I got out my keycard from my purse and waved it over the sensor.

"Like in a hotel?" Carolina asked.

"Steve says it's safer, we can change the cards whenever we want instead of having to call a locksmith."

"Safety's that much of a concern?"

"Karen's famous. That always attracts a few crazies."

She nodded, though I couldn't tell if she was simply agreeing with me, or if this was confirmation of something she'd long suspected.

We walked inside, the door closing on its own behind us. Because the house was so large, yet all on one ground floor, the foyer felt like the mouth of a cave.

What did it look like to Carolina? I had lived here most of my life, I could navigate its hallways with my eyes closed. What was she noticing her first time here?

She was looking at the walls. Karen's paintings were hung everywhere. The still lifes, the peaceful meadows, all rendered in watercolors so gentle that you wanted to take them off the canvas and wrap yourself in them, like blankets. She started walking past them, slowly, taking each one in, like she was at an art gallery back in Manhattan. I set her luggage on the floor and watched as she made the rounds. When she stopped in front of one painting, arms folded across her chest, head cocked to one side, I went over and spoke to her, softly, so as not to break the mood.

"This is one of my favorites. She painted it only a few years after the accident. It was a real breakthrough for her, figuring out how to use the talent the Lord had given her."

This was the standard line given to visitors. Usually Nancy was the one who gave it, however. Saying it myself felt exciting, and a little scary, like I was breaking a rule. An unspoken one.

The painting showed a gentle stream running through a field full of wildflowers. In the background, snow-capped mountains rose toward the sky.

"Is this nearby?" she asked.

I didn't understand. After I didn't respond for a few moments, she turned and saw the puzzled look on my face.

"Where is this place that she painted, is what I meant. Is it here? Does she roll her wheelchair out into these fields?"

"Oh, it's not a real place," I said, relieved that I finally understood. "Karen doesn't paint real places. They're glimpses of heaven, she calls them. When she goes home to the Lord and he fixes her body up like new, this is where she's going to take her first walk."

This was another of Nancy's lines. It was thrilling to deliver it. I wanted to give all of her usual speeches to Carolina. I didn't want Nancy's voice in her head, telling Karen's story. I wanted mine.

"It's a fantasy?" she asked.

"It's not a made-up place. Karen gets these glimpses of what the Lord's Kingdom is going to look like, and she paints them so other believers can look forward to what they have in store. Life down here gets hard, but it gets easier when you have an idea of what life up there is going to be like."

Carolina turned back to the painting. She tilted her head to the other side, considered it from that angle for another moment, then said, "How does she get these glimpses?"

"They're not dreams, if that's what you're thinking," I said, anticipating a common reaction. "In secular terms, you'd call it inspiration. All artists get their inspiration from the Lord, after all.

It's just that most don't have him listed in their contacts. When Karen gets a message, she knows who it is."

"She receives texts from God?"

"No, of course not, that's just an analogy we use to help people understand. God doesn't need a data plan!"

Nancy always got a laugh from that line. Carolina, however, stayed quiet.

I wanted to tell her everything about Karen. I never got the chance to do it. So when I heard footsteps coming down the south hallway, I got nervous, as if Nancy knew what I was thinking and was coming to take the reins from me.

But it wasn't Nancy. The footsteps were too heavy.

As soon as Steve entered, the foyer got smaller. He always had that effect. He was imposing, broad-shouldered and bald-headed, looking like the nightclub bouncer he used to be. But when he worked security, he had always kept to the background, arms crossed at his waist, impassive look on his face, ready to step in as soon as he was needed. He didn't do that anymore. He got in people's faces. He had to, he said. It was the only way he could do his job.

As Steve approached, Carolina uncrossed her arms and extended her right hand, ready to shake his. That wasn't how Steve did introductions, though.

I should have prepared her, told her what to expect. All I could manage to get out was a brief identification, and even then I couldn't finish it.

"Carolina, this is Steve Royce. He's Karen's soulguard and he'll—"

He brushed past me on his way to Carolina. She was still holding out her hand, and he bumped into it like a downhill skier knocking over a flag as he went out of bounds. He came to within a few inches of her face, well past the boundary of personal space she expected others to recognize. He raised his arms and placed his hands on her cheeks, drawing her toward him like she was a cantaloupe he was inspecting for ripeness. She was paralyzed. She couldn't even retract her arm, and her hand had landed on his belly like she was a doctor checking his liver.

Steve looked into her eyes. No, he looked through them. That's what it felt like, I remembered. Steve didn't inspect me very often, only when I went on trips where he wasn't able to accompany us, and when he did, it was no more annoying than having airport security ask you to take off your jewelry so they could wave the wand over you. But this was the first time Carolina had had her soul inspected, and she hadn't even had the chance to brace herself.

Would she be angry at me?

I took a step back and watched Steve scan her for any trace of demonic contamination. His examination was especially throrough, and not without reason. She was new here, for one thing, and the house had already been penetrated once. In the last few weeks, he'd been more vigilant than I had ever seen him.

He let go of her face, suddenly, like it had just become very warm. Carolina's legs fell out from under her, and she landed on the floor in a crouch. She was breathing heavily, like a diver coming up for air.

"She's clean," said Steve. He didn't address it to Carolina, and he didn't address it to me, either. The Holy Spirit was always with him when he did inspections, and he spoke to it like they were buddies in a cop movie.

I rushed over to help her up, but she held out her hand for me to stay back. Was she going to hold this against me?

"Show her to her room," Steve told me.

He left. Carolina let me take her arm and help her up. Once she was standing, though, she made me hand over all of her luggage.

"Where's my room?" she asked, forceful.

I started leading her down the east hallway, but she didn't want me to come with her.

"Just tell me where it is."

She was going to hold it against me.

I told her that her room was the third door on the left. She headed that way, the casters of her suitcase clacking on the floor.

"I'll come get you for dinner!" I called out. She didn't respond.

I heard the door slam shut. I was alone in the foyer. Had I already failed? Would she still help us?

Would she be my friend?

3

I was pacing my bedroom, bouncing off the walls like a pinball. I couldn't calm down. I tried sitting down and opening the Word, reading one of Karen's favorite passages from First Corinthians.

"Now if the foot should say, 'Because I am not a hand, I do not belong to the body,' it would not for that reason stop being part of the body. And if the ear should say, 'Because I am not an eye, I do not belong to the body,' it would not for that reason stop being part of the body. If the whole body were an eye, where would the sense of hearing be? If the whole body were an ear, where would the sense of smell be? But in fact God has placed the parts in the body, every one of them, just as he wanted them to be. If they were all one part, where would the body be? As it is, there are many parts, but one body."

My eyes skittered across the words like stones skipping across a lake.

I couldn't think of anything else. I knelt down at the foot of my bed and tried to pray.

I hardly ever prayed on my own. I know that sounds terrible. I was surrounded by genuine prayer warriors in my daily life. You'd think I would have learned a little something, but it had the opposite effect. Karen could pray so beautifully, and Steve could pray so fiercely, that I felt like I couldn't measure up. I know that doesn't matter—the Lord listens to our prayers even if we don't have the gift of eloquence—but my brain can't seem to tell that to my heart. Whenever I try to tell the Lord what I'm feeling, I think I sound stupid, like a little girl asking God to have the cute boy in class pay attention to me. So I just let others pray for me. There's always someone praying in this house, so it works out.

But when I knelt down at the foot of my bed, I felt the words pour out of my heart like it was a glass of milk that had been knocked over, spilling all over the table and onto the floor. I don't even know if "words" is the right term for what came out of me. Afterward, I could remember very little of what I said. But I remembered what I felt, along with a few images that flashed through my head, like I wasn't praying, but dreaming.

I saw myself walking across a beach. The sand was cool and wet between my toes. I looked down at my feet and noticed there was another pair of feet beside me, walking steadily, matching my pace. I looked up to see who it was.

Carolina.

She was smiling. I smiled back. She began talking, or at least her lips began moving, forming words without making a sound. I couldn't make out what she was saying. I grew frustrated. I asked her to speak up, but even though I felt my own lips move, I couldn't hear my own voice.

Then I sensed something. I didn't see or hear it. I felt it. A presence. Is that what a sixth sense is? How you perceive things in dreams?

The presence was behind us. Was that what she was trying to tell me? I began to turn around to see what it was, but I couldn't move my head. My neck was locked in place. I couldn't look away from Carolina's face. She was still talking, and I still couldn't hear her.

The presence was getting closer. I was no longer interested in finding out what it was. I just wanted to get away.

I was able to move my arm. I reached out and took Carolina's hand. I tried to run, but she wouldn't change her pace. We needed to move. I tugged on her arm, but she wouldn't respond, as if she couldn't sense the presence that was bearing down on us.

A sound filled the whole beach. A sound like a heartbeat.

Sometimes, a sound in the real world will be incorporated into a dream. An alarm clock becomes the sound of a fast-approaching train. This is what happened to me. The sound that sounded like a heartbeat in my dream was the sound of someone knocking on my door in the real world. After a few more knocks,

I snapped out of the dream. But I didn't get up to answer it, not at first. I was still figuring out what had happened.

Had I been praying? If so, had I experienced a vision, similar to the glimpses of heaven Karen received? I wanted to ask her about it, but I didn't know how to put it into words. Maybe I had simply fallen asleep and the whole thing was a dream, my brain trying to process what had happened?

These thoughts rattled around my head as I stood up and answered the door. When I opened it, I calmed down.

Carolina stood in the doorway.

"Can I come in for a second?" she said.

"Yes, of course. Have a seat."

She came into my room and sat down in my chair, crossing her legs so that it looked like she was levitating. I sat down on my bed like we were best friends talking about what had happened at school.

"I'm sorry about Steve," I said.

"Does he always do that?" she asked.

"Not always, but he's been extra careful the last few months."

"It'll make for a good detail."

"Steve would be perfect for your story. He's got a story of his own."

"You want to tell it? Here, let me get it on record."

She took out her phone and placed it on the desk, directing it toward me. She hit record and waited for me to start.

What would Nancy think of that?

I knew what she would think. I did it anyway.

Steve Royce used to be a bouncer in New York nightclubs. He was known throughout the city as one of the toughest there was, one who wouldn't hesitate to break someone's arm to keep things in order. His reputation was enough to get him noticed by the nightclub's clients. One of them, a singer who had sold millions of records, liked Steve's style so much he hired him as his personal bodyguard. Steve traveled with the singer all over the world, handling security.

More than security, in fact. Whatever the singer wanted, Steve provided it. Women, drugs. Steve did it all. There was nothing he hadn't seen.

When the singer was performing in Memphis, Steve arranged for a private party at the singer's hotel room. He used his local contacts to get everything the singer wanted, all the lusts of the flesh. He gave them the name of the hotel and where they should go when they arrived: room 416.

As the party got underway, Steve went downstairs to the lobby to handle payment for the girls that were in attendance. When he was done, he got on the elevator and headed back up.

That was when he made a mistake. The one that saved his life.

He accidentally hit the button for the third floor. Not the fourth. He walked down the hallway, which looked exactly the same as the hallway on the fourth floor. He came to the room where the party was happening. Only it was a different room.

Room 316.

He tried his keycard, but it didn't work. He tried it a few more times, then knocked on the door. And by the grace of God, who so loved the world that He gave His only son, someone answered.

Karen.

She was in town to speak at a conference. She and Nancy were staying at the same hotel.

It was Nancy who opened the door. Steve saw he had the wrong room and apologized. He was about to leave when a voice from inside the room called out, telling him to come in. Steve said he had somewhere to be, but the voice insisted. Steve went in.

When he saw Karen in her wheelchair, he didn't know what to say. When Karen saw him, however, she knew exactly what to say.

She called out in the name of the Lord.

Steve asked what she thought she was doing.

Karen said he was trapped in a web of sinfulness and debauchery.

Steve said he didn't know what she was talking about.

Karen said he knew exactly what she was talking about, that the fate of his soul was at stake and he had to act. Now.

She exhorted him to turn away from his life of sin. Steve grew more and more angry, telling Karen to mind her own business. This went on and on, Karen raising her voice, Steve raising his, until Steve was shouting so loudly his face was turning red. In the middle of shouting, he clutched his throat as if he couldn't breathe. He fell to his knees, asking Karen to call for help. But she stayed where she was.

He passed out. He lay on the ground for he didn't know how long. But when he came to, he knew what he had to do.

He begged Karen to ask God for forgiveness. He crawled forward on his knees, approaching her wheelchair. He pleaded with her to help him.

She told him that forgiveness wasn't hers to give, but God's. He simply had to ask for it.

Broken, Steve prayed to God, asking for forgiveness. When he received it, he felt as if he had woken from a dream. He turned to Karen and thanked her. She said that she was simply the Lord's instrument. Well then, Steve wanted to show this instrument his appreciation.

He leaned down to her foot. He brought his lips to her ankle. And kissed it.

He's been with us ever since, protecting Karen from whatever threatened her. Until he couldn't.

Carolina hit stop.

How long had I been speaking? Time had stepped into the background and I had lost track of it.

"When I was flying over here, I didn't think there would be a story here for me to tell. Now I think there might be."

"We can't wait to see what you do! Maybe you can include Steve's story and get help for others who are lost."

"You keep saying I'm going to help you. How am I supposed to do that?"

The heartbeat sound again. Someone else was at the door, knocking. But not to ask me to open it. This was a knock to let me know that someone was coming in, whether or not I let her.

It was Nancy.

Nancy is my mother, but that's not how I think of her. She's Nancy, Karen's manager. When I stop and think of how I relate to her, I realize I think of myself as Nancy's assistant more than her daughter. Her job is who she is. But it's not like some executive who spends all night at the office, never seeing her loved ones. For Nancy, doing her job is her way of being with the people she loves. There's no one in the world she cares about more than Karen. More than me, even. It doesn't bother me, though. Nancy's love for Karen has always been inspiring to me, the devoted love of a sister in Christ.

She was wearing dressy jeans, a white tailored oxford shirt, and a black blazer with navy and white lining. She always dressed better than me. If I wanted to know how to dress better, I could have asked her, but that felt like I would have been breaking a rule, a daughter asking her mother for fashion advice. When I had bought my scarf, I had done it alone, without her even knowing. This was the first time she'd even seen it. The main idea was to have something nice to wear while picking up Carolina, but I'd also wanted to impress Nancy.

She did little more than glance at me, however. She was too busy introducing herself to Carolina. This was her job, and she was good at it.

"Carolina, so wonderful to meet you," said Nancy, walking inside and extending her hand. Following Steve's soul-inspection, Carolina was still reluctant about making physical contact, but Nancy was so personable that she couldn't help but offer her hand. Nancy sensed that Steve had shaken her up, so she went the extra mile to make sure she felt welcomed.

"Hannah was just getting me acclimated," said Carolina.

"Don't worry, I haven't told her where the bodies are buried."

Had I just made a joke? I never made jokes. Nancy knew that about me, and there was a look of shock on her face for a second. Carolina started laughing, however, and I joined in. Nancy didn't want to be left out, so she laughed along with us, though she didn't see what was so funny.

"We're all very excited to see what you have in store," said Nancy. "The minute your editor contacted us, I just knew this was going to work out."

"You were the one communicating with my editor?"

"I handle all of Karen's PR responsibilities."

"What did she tell you about what I had in mind? I just want to make sure we're on the same page."

"What do we have in mind? You're from Browsr! We want to do what you always do."

I had only met Carolina this morning, but I knew her well enough to recognize when she was annoyed. She gave a small, tight smile and nodded slightly. She looked like an emoticon.

"We can talk over all this during dinner. I know Karen will be interested to hear your thoughts on how to go forward."

"Me too."

The dining room was the nerve center of the house. When visitors came to see Karen, this was where they were introduced to her. The dining table was a large oval, and on the left was a notch where Karen rolled up. It looked like someone had taken a bite out of a potato chip. On the walls were photographs of some of the people who had come to visit: authors, politicians, even a few celebrities. There was one celebrity, a woman with her own reality show. She had visited a few years ago, bringing along her camera crew. Nancy had long meetings with them to determine how they were going to portray Karen. In fact, Nancy had wanted to get Karen her own show on the same network as the celebrity. But those plans had fallen through, and though she didn't say it outright, I think it was because Nancy had been too demanding. When it came to Karen, there was nothing she wouldn't do. She said that herself.

Carolina and I sat on the far side of the table, opposite Karen's notch. Steve sat to the right, Nancy to the left. Steve made no mention of putting his hands on Carolina. For him, there was nothing to apologize for. But Carolina looked at him warily, like she was ready to grab her butter knife and defend herself if he tried anything. He gave no indication that he noticed how she was eyeing him, but I knew he was aware. He noticed everything.

"Let's have her meet you," said Nancy.

She stood up, me and Steve following her example. We had done this countless times, and had the choreography down flat. Nancy wanted to make sure guests didn't feel anything like pity when they saw Karen. She wanted them to be in awe.

Carolina saw that we were all standing and roused herself from the chair like a teenager dragging her feet as she followed family protocol. But when Karen entered, she stood up straight.

Karen's wheelchair was electric. She controlled it manually, or rather, pedally: there was a joystick set up at her foot, which she operated with her toes. Her foot was the first thing you saw when entered the room. The chair had a leg for her leg, holding it up like the arm of a crane. The rest of the chair came into the room and you saw Karen lying more than sitting, the odd angle helping her extend her foot as far as possible. But she didn't seem bedridden, unable to function. She looked like a queen, servants and machinery performing the mundane activities that were beneath her station.

We were all silent as she wheeled over to her notch on the opposite side of the table. She was silent too, knowing that she didn't need to do anything else to command our attention. She arranged her chair at an acute angle to the table, like a business executive brandishing her elbow on the table during the big meeting.

She didn't acknowledge the rest of us. She looked straight at Carolina.

"Welcome, sister," she said.

We all sat down. Carolina synchronized with the rest of us.

We were brought our meals. A local chef often came here for these more formal occasions. He specialized in high-end, lo-cal versions of the comfort foods Karen and Nancy knew from their childhoods in Ohio. Karen waited until all of us had been given our plate of lemongrass coleslaw before she spoke.

"I prefer to make first impressions during a meal rather than a meeting. The Lord instructs us to break bread with each other."

"To break bread with one's friends, or one's enemies?" said Carolina.

What was she doing? Starting the meal by acting defensive? Was this a journalistic tactic they taught at secular universities?

"You don't consider yourself an enemy, do you?"

"Everyone has been treating me like a friend, and I don't know why. It's made me wonder what else I might be."

"Has Hannah done something?" asked Nancy.

My throat went dry. What would she say? If she mentioned that I had told her about Karen's condition, would Nancy get angry with me, keeping me away from Carolina during the rest of her stay?

"Hannah has been nothing but friendly."

I let out a sigh. Nancy noticed it.

"But the way she's talked about my assignment makes me wonder if there hasn't been some misunderstanding."

"What's been misunderstood?" said Nancy.

"Me," said Carolina.

"I told you we shouldn't have invited the secular media," said Steve.

24

Karen made a shushing gesture with her foot. It sounds strange, but her foot is incredibly expressive. She can convey the full range of body language with just an ankle and five little toes, as if her foot is a highly intricate marionette that can express every last nuance.

"Let me be honest. This won't work unless all of us are honest about our intentions."

Karen wheeled back from the table, making it easier for her and Carolina to maintain eye contact.

"I am experiencing a great struggle. The greatest of my life. I've withdrawn from my usual engagements because I don't believe my audience would understand the nature of it, no matter how sympathetic they might be. I was prepared to face this struggle and combat the Accuser in private, but then we received the message from your editor."

"She seemed to know what was going on," said Nancy. "And she wasn't judgmental, like some others have been. She was simply curious."

Nancy gave a quick glance when she made that last remark. Steve snorted and shook his head.

"Nancy told me about some of the stories Browsr does. Providing help to the afflicted, explaining unusual struggles to a wide audience and making them comprehensible. I'm not too proud to admit that I need any help you can offer."

Everyone regarded Carolina, waiting to hear what she had to say. Especially me.

"You think I'm here to do a spiritual makeover?"

"That's one way of putting it, yes."

"I'm not from a newsmagazine. This isn't a feel-good prime-time special. I'm a serious journalist. Browsr has one of the largest staffs of reporters and editors in the industry."

"And you write about cats," said Nancy.

Carolina glared at her. She had largely restrained her emotions since arriving, and seeing her unleash them at their full force was thrilling.

"I'm sorry, I don't mean to offend. But that is what you do, right? Funny lists, feel-good articles? This is what I see on Facebook. We thought you wanted to do something like that."

"If you want to bring in some specialists, even an exorcist, I'd be willing to go along," said Karen.

"Carolina is Catholic," I said.

Nancy and Karen both found this encouraging. Steve looked disgusted. And Carolina looked betrayed.

Did she not understand I was speaking up for her?

This had happened before. People thought I was on their side until I opened my mouth. I needed to get better at keeping quiet.

"So you're familiar with spiritual warfare?" said Karen.

"Catholicism is nothing but idolatry!" said Steve.

"Maybe that's just what we need," said Nancy.

"I'm not going to chant any rosaries," said Carolina. "I'm a lapsed Catholic, the only worthwhile kind there is. I have sex. I smoke weed. I don't believe any of this."

"But you're still here," said Karen.

"Not for long."

She pushed her chair back from the table. I grabbed hold of her wrist, trying to keep her here, but she shook me off. She was about to get up and leave, and she would have if it hadn't happened. In an odd way, I'm glad it did.

I hadn't actually seen it. Nancy and Steve had worked hard to keep Karen isolated from me and everyone else, but I had heard them talk about it and could hear the fear in their voices. But nothing could have prepared me for witnessing it in the flesh.

Her foot, her gift from the Lord, began to spasm like a fish that had been snatched out of the water and cast onto dry land. But a fish would have begun to slow down and grow exhausted as the life left it. The spasms only grew worse, more contorted, more horrid, as if it wasn't dying but being transformed into another creature. The toes, the ankle, the heel, they twisted and writhed, the movements entirely alien to a human limb.

I tore my eyes away from the foot only to see Karen's face. She was completely, utterly terrified. Her eyes bulged, her lips went white. Seeing her face make such unfamiliar expressions was almost as unnerving as seeing her foot jerk and flail.

Karen opened her mouth, and if she screamed, I didn't hear it. But I think she made some sort of sound, because Steve leapt up and grabbed hold of her foot, saying to steady it, only to jump back as if he had touched a live electrical wire. Nancy shouted at us, pointing at the door and telling us to get out. I couldn't move, but Carolina took me by the arm and lifted me up, dragging me out of the dining room as I bumped my knees on the legs of the dining room chairs. The pain was almost pleasant, like grass on my bare feet.

4

I woke up in my room. The lights were off. I thought I sensed that someone else was in there with me, but when I turned on the lamp on my nightstand, the room was empty.

I checked the time on my phone. 3:00. After I had blacked out during dinner, I must have slept through the rest of the evening.

I peeled back the covers and sat up. I got out of bed, slipping into my fuzzy slippers. I opened the door and padded down the hallway to the living room.

Nancy and Steve both had smartphones that could get on the internet, but all I had was a flip phone. I couldn't have a laptop in my bedroom. If I wanted to go online, I had to use the computer in the living room. It's not like Steve looked over my shoulder as I checked Facebook—often I had the living room to myself—but I still had to be deliberate about it. I couldn't just get on for a few minutes while I was standing in line at the supermarket.

I sat in the chair and woke up the computer. The house was so quiet that I could hear it whirr into wakefulness.

I didn't go to Facebook, though. I went to the Browsr site. I went to the search bar and typed in Carolina's full name. I got a dozen or so returns, the lists and GIF sets she'd put together. I found the one I was looking for.

"17 Virgines de Guadalupe Who Can't Even."

Each entry showed a Virgen sitting on a shelf or in someone's home. They all had unusual expressions, as if they were looking beyond the frame at something strange or troubling. Below was a funny caption, the Virgen speaking in a text-speak so full of slang and acronyms that I barely understood it.

I opened another tab and Googled "Virgen de Guadalupe," copy-and-pasting it from Browsr to make sure I got the spelling right. I read the Wikipedia entry, looked at the images of T-shirts and tattoos. I'd heard stories of the Virgin Mary appearing to people in potato chips and tortillas, but those were little more than jokes. This was a whole history, one story getting told and retold by different people in different times and places.

Almost 500 years ago, a farmer named Juan Diego was walking on a hill in Mexico when an image of the Virgen appeared to him. He went and told the local priest, who didn't believe him. The Virgen would never appear to a farmer, the priest told him. Juan Diego went back to the hill and the Virgen appeared again. This time, he asked her for a sign. The Virgen told him to turn around. Juan Diego saw that a bed of roses had grown right there in the middle of winter. He gathered up the roses in his cloak and ran down to show the priest. When he opened his cloak, the roses fell onto the ground and formed an image of the Virgen, the same one Juan Diego had seen on the hilltop. The priest couldn't help but be convinced by the miracle.

The priest hadn't believed at first, so the message had needed to be adapted. Is this what we needed to do?

I heard footsteps. I didn't want to speak to anyone. I started to get up from the desk, but I needed to turn off the computer. I didn't want anyone to know I had been on it, much less what I'd been searching for. I managed to close all the tabs, but wasn't able to make an escape. Nancy came into the living room. It was five in the morning, and she was already dressed for the day.

I was worried she would ask what I was doing on the computer, but she didn't even acknowledge it. Instead, she simply started talking like she was resuming a conversation I didn't know we'd been having.

"Karen doesn't understand what's going on, you know."

"You mean her foot's fine?"

"No, there's something wrong with it, but not what she thinks. Steve's the one filling her head with this nonsense about demons. What Karen really has is something called body dysmorphic disorder. It's a condition where you think part of your body—the foot, oftentimes—doesn't belong to you. Like someone else has put it there. Makes you go crazy. I looked it up on the internet. Is that what you were checking?"

"Yes," I said. First I was making jokes, and now I was telling lies. What was happening to me? "You should tell her about this. We could do it together."

"I have, many times. Steve just calls me an unbeliever."

"Couldn't you get a doctor to come and visit? Wouldn't he agree with you?"

"You think she'd listen to a doctor? She thought Carolina would have known how to proceed. Now that hope is gone, and she doesn't know what to do."

Nancy knelt down. She put her hand on my shoulder. She was never like this with me.

"You're the one who has to save her. This is what you were born for. This is why God gave you to me."

She raised her hand from my shoulder to my cheek. She stroked it for a moment, looking into my eyes, then stood up and left.

Something was wrong with Karen, but was something wrong with Nancy too? She never spoke to me like that. Her love and affection for me, I knew, were always implicit. She never had to spell it out. Why was she doing that now?

I was so distracted that it took me several moments to notice the shushing sound coming from behind me.

"Psst!"

It was Carolina. She was trying to get my attention without coming into the living room, where Nancy might notice her. I got up from the desk and walked over to her.

"Let's get out of here," I said.

She misunderstood me. She thought I was taking her to the airport so she could catch the earliest flight out of here, but I just needed to get out of the house. She was disappointed, but still relieved to get away.

We went to a Starbucks. I ordered two pumpkin spice lattes. When we sat down, I told her what Nancy had told me. She had several questions, but not about Karen or Nancy. She wanted to know about me.

"You and Nancy have lived with Karen your whole lives?"

"She takes care of us."

"Can I ask how old you are?"

"Thirty-two."

A look of shock came across her face. She didn't even try to hide it.

"I'm sorry, I just thought you were my age."

"You did?"

I had never felt the same age as my friends—when I had friends. I was young but I seemed old, or I was old but I seemed young. I'd come to accept that I would always be out of step with people who were supposed to be my peers. But having Carolina think we were the same age, that we could be roommates or work lousy jobs in the big city, was a surprise. My second of the day, and it wasn't even lunch.

"I've grown up differently than most people, I know. Karen's been my life. I didn't go to school. Nancy homeschooled me when I was younger, but by the time I was a teenager, being Karen's assistant was a full-time job."

"What did your dad think of this?"

I didn't answer.

"I'm sorry, I'm prying," she said.

"You're a journalist, aren't you?"

"I suppose I am."

So I told her.

When Karen had her accident, Nancy was devastated. She was so upset that she ran away from home. On the night she sat on the diving board and prayed to God, Karen felt the twinge in her foot. But Nancy didn't know that. She got up from the diving board, went into the house, packed a few things, and left. With all the excitement about Karen regaining feeling in her foot, no one noticed Nancy was gone.

All told, she was gone for three months. Her family called the police, got in contact with other church leaders, trying to find a lead. One youth pastor in Tennessee had seen her. She'd appeared in town with a boy, a former member of the youth pastor's Wednesday night meetings. But she was only in town for one day.

They kept looking for her, calling churches all across the region. They didn't find any more leads, but they didn't have to. One night, exactly three months after she had disappeared, Nancy came back. Karen's father found her at the pool, sitting on the diving board, as though she'd never left.

She wouldn't say much about where she had been. She still doesn't, in fact. When the Lord forgives you, you could forget about it, as she liked to say. All she really said was she ran off to Tennessee, found this boy she had met at a conference, and took off with him. She wouldn't say where they had gone, or what they had done. Her family didn't question her too much. They were just grateful to have her back. There was one thing, however, that she couldn't not talk about.

She was pregnant.

The boy she ran off with, that's my father. I've never met him. I've never wanted to.

She had the baby. Me, that is. She could have easily given me up. Karen's family had lots of connections with Christian adoption agencies, but as soon as I was born, it energized her. And it's not just Nancy saying that. Everyone noticed it. Taking care of me, she found a strength she didn't know she had, and she used that strength to take care of Karen, too. She saw God's plan clearly: if she had only had Karen to take care of, she couldn't have done it; if she had only had me to take care of, she couldn't have done it; but having the both of us to take care of was exactly what she needed to keep herself going. The Bible says that God will never give us any more than we can handle in life. As Nancy says, He also never gives us any less.

Carolina didn't record me, but she didn't need to. She listened to me so attentively that I felt like she was reading, my story already set down on paper for her to study. She would be able to recite it word for word, if she had to.

"That's my story, but I don't know if it explains anything. Besides how isolated and backward I am."

"You're still so articulate about it. People with experiences like yours, they can't always do that."

"It's because I have you to talk to. When you listen to me, I can put things into words that I never could otherwise."

She leaned back in her chair. I had said too much, shown how desperate I was to have her as my friend. I needed to think of something that would show I wasn't crazy, or at least not as crazy as Karen and Nancy.

"You still looking for people to interview?"

"What's the point? That's not why Karen asked me here."

"But you're still here. Can't you make a good story out of us?"

Her interest in me was starting to turn into pity. But at least I had her attention.

"Who did you have in mind?"

"I thought you might want to meet Karen's family."

5

There were two kinds of people in Colorado: Christians and hippies. I knew all about the former, just a little bit about the latter. Nancy liked to shop at a clothing store run by a woman who always talked about her chakras and how Mercury was in retrograde. I was too intimidated to accompany her.

Many different ministries operated here, drawn by the abundance of God's natural beauty the state offered. It was one of the reasons why Karen had chosen to make her home here. She wasn't the only one, either; her parents lived here as well.

Les and Lisa Wallin lived in a condo on the opposite end of town, near the restaurant district. Les was the director of a Christian counseling center, a job he had acquired through his daughter's connections with the local evangelical community. They were like grandparents to me, even more than my actual grandparents. Nancy's mother and father had gotten divorced soon after I was born, moving away from Ohio in opposite directions. But Les and Lisa more than made up for their absence. Les used to take me on grandfather-granddaughter dates when I was a little girl, going to the movies or riding go-karts.

Come to think of it, I hadn't gone on any dates since, grandfather or otherwise.

The condo was bright and spacious, meant to accommodate guests. For the last few months, it had been accommodating one guest in particular: Karen's husband, Mitch Kerry.

Mitch was the worship director at Stone Garden Church where all of us attended. It had more than 5,000 members, three services every Sunday morning. He had met Karen when she spoke there several years ago. They were both in their 40s, committed to being single and doing the work of the Lord, but once they met, well, that was that. They were married a few months later. Karen wrote a book about the experience of falling in love with a godly man, and it went on to become her bestselling book.

What neither of them had publicized, however, was the fact that they were no longer living together.

Mitch had moved out shortly before Karen began suffering from demonic possession. Or body dysmorphic disorder. I didn't know the details of their separation, though Nancy implied that Mitch was frustrated with Karen's physical condition and had started having an affair. I couldn't imagine that, though. Mitch was devoted to Karen. Whatever the reason, he had moved out. Karen, along with the pastoral team at Stone Garden, had suggested that he live at Karen's parents' house during the separation. Her father was a trained counselor and would be able to guide his son-in-law through this difficult time.

"It would be worthwhile to interview Mitch," I said as we sat in the driveway. "Les and Lisa too, if you want to know more about Karen's childhood."

"He's staying with the parents of the woman he's separated from?"

"He's still a part of Karen's family. This could help keep it that way."

This was how Les and Lisa had described it to me, and I'd thought it sounded reasonable. But the look on Carolina's face made it clear she found it strange.

Lisa answered the door, gathering me into a long, close hug. She was one of those grandmothers who stayed so fit and healthy she seemed younger than people half her age. Nancy sometimes thought she was overdoing it, as if she were making up for the physical activity her daughter couldn't perform. But I had always known Lisa wasn't trying to show up Karen. She was trying to be remarkable in her own way. Karen's grace and authority came so naturally, but Lisa had to work for it, and for far less recognition. I knew just how she felt.

I stepped back from Lisa's hug and introduced her to Carolina.

"So glad you're here! We just know you're going to be able to help out our Karen."

"Nice to meet you," said Carolina, avoiding the subject of Karen entirely.

We sat in the living room. The furniture was white and there were many windows for letting in natural light. Carolina blinked and squinted for a few moments before getting used to it.

Lisa said she would get us some fresh-squeezed orange juice. We heard her in the kitchen, sounding like she was tuning a bicycle.

While we were waiting, Les came out of his office. He moved through the living room like it was a stage. He sat on the loveseat perpendicular to the couch where Carolina and I were sitting. He gave Carolina the story he thought she was here for, how he first felt when Karen had the accident, how proud he was of the rest of her recovery, how he continued to be amazed at the ways the Lord was working in her life, making her ministry thrive and grow.

I had heard it all before, so I didn't listen to Les' words so much as the sound of his voice. There was something about it I couldn't quite explain, as if it were the melody of a song whose words I couldn't remember.

He stopped. I looked over to see that Les had asked me a question, and both he and Carolina were waiting for my answer.

"I'm sorry?" I said.

"He asked why we came over," said Carolina.

"Other than to say hello!" said Les.

I leaned forward and said, "We want to speak to Mitch."

If the living room was a stage, then Les expected visitors to stick to the script. I was improvising.

"Mitch is in a very sensitive place right now. I don't know that it would be best for a stranger to disturb him."

I'd thought it would be best for me to ask. If Carolina had requested to see Mitch, Les might have accused her of sowing discord during a difficult family situation. But it turned out she knew just what to say. She was a real journalist, after all.

"Did Karen tell you why I came out here?" she said.

"You were going to help her, then write a story about it and help other people."

"If I'm going to help her, I need to know what's going on in her life."

"What makes you think you're going to help her?"

"Sometimes you need to bring in someone new. They might see something that others have missed."

Though he didn't show it, I knew Les was furious. He didn't like having his expertise questioned, especially by an unbelieving young woman.

"You love your daughter, don't you?"

"How dare you ask me that?"

"Prove it, then. Let me try to help."

He turned to me. "You've allowed this to cross your threshold?"

"It was already there," I said.

He shook his head and looked out the window. "Do what you will," he said.

Lisa came in from the kitchen bearing our glasses of fresh-squeezed orange juice on a tray, but Les caught her eye and shook his head. She returned to the kitchen and poured the juice down the sink.

Les had had the basement converted into a separate residence with its own entrance. I led Carolina around back.

"You told him you were going to help Karen," I said.

"You saying I lied?"

"I'm just saying it worked."

She had been scowling, but she stopped and gave me a little forgiving nod. Maybe I could still salvage the situation.

Before I knocked on the door, I checked my phone.

"Something up?" Carolina said.

"No, it's fine."

I knocked. Mitch couldn't have been expecting guests, but he still didn't seem surprised to see us.

Mitch was very good-looking. He had released several albums of praise-and-worship music, his lightly stubbled face on the covers. A few congregants had even said he was too handsome to lead worship, his attractiveness a potential stumbling block that might cause women, those weaker vessels, to dwell upon his physical attributes rather than God's glory. But he didn't look all that attractive in the guesthouse. His stubble had grown to an unruly beard, obscuring his features, and he was wearing sweatpants and an old church t-shirt that highlighted his growing paunch.

He led us inside without asking us what we wanted. He had us sit at the small dining table in the kitchenette and went to get something from the refrigerator. A beer. He sat at the table and brandished the bottle like a switchblade.

"Want one?" he asked.

I shook my head. I was about to explain what we were doing here, but Carolina quickly took the lead. Being around Mitch made her feel as comfortable as she had been since getting here. Not that he was warm or kind. Just the opposite, in fact. But he knew something was wrong and wasn't pretending otherwise. Just the kind of person who would give a good interview.

Carolina made her introductions, set her phone on the table and hit record. Mitch regarded it like he was kneeling in a confessional booth.

"You left Karen around the same time that she first started showing symptoms, correct?"

"Symptoms of what? There's nothing wrong with her other than the fact that she always wants attention. You coming here, writing a story about her, that's exactly what she wants."

"You don't believe she's possessed by demons?"

"The only thing more ridiculous than that story is Nancy's

claim that it's some kind of psychological condition."

"Body dysmorphic disorder?" I said. "She told you about that?"

"She went looking on the internet for a story and found just what she needed. I wouldn't be surprised if this was all her idea."

"Why would she do that?" Carolina said.

"Karen's not as popular as she used to be. She hasn't had a bestseller since our love at first sight book. Her readers took that as a happy ending and stopped paying attention. People don't want to know what happens after the fairy tale ends. This demon horseshit is just what she needs to sell a million copies."

"So why did she have Carolina come out here? Why not write the book herself?" I said.

"No one would believe her if she were the only one telling the story. But if someone from the secular media came along, acting skeptical and trying to debunk her claims of the supernatural, people would come to her defense. Your level-headed appeals to reason were exactly the ammunition she needed."

Could Karen be this paranoid? I couldn't imagine it. But I also couldn't imagine her and Mitch ever splitting up.

I looked at my phone again. I put it back.

"You're separated right now," said Carolina. "Are you going to file for divorce?"

"Am I going to break the promise I made before God and thus ruin my career in the Christian music industry? Les and Lisa are trying to get me to see the error of my ways and return to my loving wife. But I'm thinking of getting into country music. They're God-fearing folk, but they understand when you fuck up. Look at Vince Gill."

Mitch drained the rest of his beer in one gulp. Carolina and I got up to leave. Before I stepped out the door, Mitch laid his hand on my shoulder.

"Don't let her get to you," he said.

I nodded. I followed Carolina back to the car. Before I

turned the ignition, however, I became distracted. Who was Mitch talking about? Who shouldn't I let get to me?

6

Steve was in our faces the moment we got back.

"Where have you been? Nancy's been trying to get ahold of you."

While we were at Les and Lisa's, my phone had buzzed several times. It was Nancy. That was why I had ignored it, saying it was nothing.

"What's going on?" I asked.

"Karen's battling the Accuser. She's been asking for you."

"Me? What for?"

"Not you." Steve maintained eye contact with me while pointing at Carolina, the unwelcome third party. "Her."

Carolina grabbed my arm like she was about to lose balance. I took her by the bicep and propped her up.

"You can do this," I said.

"Do what?" she said.

"Pray on her behalf," said Steve. "Tell Satan there's no vacancy. You can even rattle your rosary beads if you want. I'm sure she'd appreciate it."

Carolina was too scared to get offended. She let Steve lead the way to Karen's bedroom. I kept holding on to her arm and placed my other hand on her shoulder, guiding her like she was a child learning to ride a bicycle.

What did I think was happening to Karen? I'd heard so many theories, and I didn't know which one to believe. Even if I did know what was wrong with here—or if there was anything wrong with her—I still thought Carolina could help. I had more faith in her than anyone else.

More than God, even?

Steve opened the door. Karen's bedroom was filled with medical equipment, monitors and apparatuses of all kinds, but it didn't feel like a hospital. It was like a hotel room, and the equipment was simply the hotel staff catering to her every need. This was by design. Karen had taken her physical impairments and turned them into demands to be met.

But that sense of order had vanished. Karen was not in control. She was lying in bed, screaming.

"GET IT OUT! GET IT OUT NOW!"

Her foot, suspended in a harness, was spasming even more violently than last night at dinner. It looked like dough kneaded by an unseen hand, lumpy and misshapen.

Nancy was standing beside the bed.

"Where were you?"

"We were visiting—"

"I don't care where you were! Just get over here!"

Carolina tensed up. I had to push her toward the bed like a statue.

"You're the one she wants to see," Nancy said. "God knows why."

Carolina couldn't look at Karen on her own. I took her head and held it against mine, like I was putting a broken finger in a splint.

It looked like Karen's face, the one that appeared on the dustjackets of her books, had been peeled off to reveal a face that was all sinew, sweat, and fear. Her eyes were wide as if held open by forceps, her pupils dilated so fully they looked like beads of mercury. She turned her head toward us. There was no recognition in her eyes when she looked at me. But when she saw Carolina, her entire head began to twitch.

"DO IT! YOU HAVE TO DO IT!"

The force of her voice made Carolina jump.

"What am I supposed to do?"

"She thought you would know," said Nancy.

"I don't even know what's going on!"

"She needs a laying on of hands," said Steve. "The demon needs to feel another claim this body."

"I should put my hand on her forehead?" said Carolina.

"Not her forehead."

We all looked at Steve, then at Carolina when we realized what he was asking of her.

She began shaking her head. I held it tight against mine to steady her.

"This is why you're here," I said.

She didn't answer.

I led her to the foot of the bed. Karen's foot hung from the harness, twitching like a flame on a wick. I took Carolina's elbows and raised her arms upward.

Her hands gripped Karen's foot like it was the handle of a roller coaster. Carolina and Karen both grimaced, the same look of something within them being torn out forcibly. Carolina's mouth twisted and her tongue jerked like a propeller.

She shouted something in a language I didn't know. I was sure that it was language, a word or phrase in some foreign tongue. The sound had too much order to be a shout or a rasp.

Carolina speaking was the last thing I remembered. After that, darkness.

I was in the bedroom. But I wasn't in bed. I was in the chair. When I had woken in the middle of the night before and felt a presence there with me, had I felt my own presence from the future?

But there was someone else in the bed. I could see the shape of a body without being able to make out its identity. I leaned over and saw Carolina's dark black hair splayed out across the pillow. She was asleep, as if she were being kept under by anesthesia. I sat back in the chair and tried to make sense of what had happened.

Something was clearly wrong with Karen. Mitch was projecting when he said this was all in her head. But what was wrong, exactly? Was it medical? Supernatural? If there was a difference, what was it?

I found I was asking myself what I believed. No one else ever did. They just assumed I believed in the same things as them, so I had to be the one to do it.

I believed there was something happening to Karen, but a demon wasn't causing it. God was. He was sending a message to Karen, and all of us, by allowing her foot to become afflicted. What was the message? I still didn't know, but I believed I wouldn't be able to figure it out on my own. That was why God had sent Carolina to us. She was the key that could decipher it.

There was also what I wanted to believe was true: that God had sent Carolina to me so I could have a friend. I hoped this was true, but I couldn't be sure.

I looked at the desk. Her laptop was there. I opened it and went on the internet to check a few things.

Carolina began stirring underneath the covers. She opened her eyes. She wasn't shocked or disturbed to see me sitting there. I thought she seemed comforted to find me there with her, but maybe I was projecting my own feelings onto her.

"What happened?" she asked, drowsy.

"I was going to ask you that."

"I touched her foot." She wasn't stating a fact so much as testing out a possibility.

"It looked like it hurt," I said.

She pulled her hand out from under the covers and looked at it. It looked the same as before. She turned it back and forth, as if she were trying on a glove, seeing how it looked.

"I said something."

"It sounded like another language. Do you think you were speaking in tongues?"

"Catholics don't go for that. Probably I was just reciting part of Mass."

"You still go?"

"When I visit my parents," she said. "I've gone a few times by myself in the city. They have such beautiful cathedrals there.

There's one in my neighborhood. St. Gregory's. Going there makes me feel like I'm going to church for the first time."

"I've never not gone to church."

"You should come to Mass with me sometime, see what you think of it."

I wanted to go with her right now. But I still had responsibilities here.

There was a knock on the door. It was Nancy.

I thought she would berate me for ignoring her calls yesterday, claiming I had missed the window to provide Karen the help she needed. But she was apologetic, as if she didn't want to bother me.

She wouldn't meet my eyes.

"Karen would like to see you," she said.

So I went to see her.

And I knew what I had to do.

7

I waited until Carolina was busy with an email to slip out the door. I got in the car and drove into town to the Home Depot. I had never been there before, but I didn't ask any of the clerks for help. I walked through the aisles like I was on autopilot until I came to what I needed. It was further confirmation that Karen was right. This is what needed to happen, and I was the one to do it.

I never would have guessed this was my purpose. Many parts, one body.

I drove back to the house. I had some difficulty carrying it inside and remaining unseen. I heard Steve coming down the hallway, but he stopped before he reached the foyer, turned around, and headed back. Was Karen keeping him occupied? Or were circumstances simply on our side?

I went to my room and took it out of its packaging. The instruction manual fell to the floor. I opened the door and peered out both ways, making sure no one saw me. I tiptoed down the hallway to the foyer, then through the back hallway to Karen's room.

I entered.

She was in her bed. Her foot was still suspended from the harness, though it wasn't moving. It looked like a sleeping animal.

"You got it," said Karen.

"Think it'll do the job?"

"I have the utmost faith in you."

Karen believing in me meant more than Carolina offering me her friendship, honestly. I felt bad thinking that, as if Carolina might be offended, but Karen is the most important person in my life. Always has been. Even when I didn't know it. Especially when I didn't know it.

"I'll do it fast," I said.

"You'll do it right. I know it."

All of the electrical outlets were taken with medical equipment. I undid one of the monitors whose function I didn't know to free up the outlet.

I plugged it in. I picked it up.

I turned on the saw.

Nancy came in almost immediately, alerted by the buzzing. She yelled at me to stop, but I ignored her. She called Steve, who stumbled into the room and pointed at me.

"Stop, I command you!"

I didn't respond. He started to approach, but I brandished the saw until he fell back to the doorway. Then I went to work.

Just before I began, however, Carolina appeared in the doorway. Our eyes met. I could see her lips move, but I couldn't hear what she was saying.

Was this the moment I had seen? Had the presence I'd sensed behind us been Karen?

No, not Karen. Not anymore. I had sensed the presence of God embodied in Karen's foot.

The fear I had experienced in my vision was gone. In its place I felt only peace. This was the support Carolina gave me, even if she didn't know it. With her support, I turned back to the task at hand.

Or foot, rather.

Did I just make another joke? I must have gained more confidence than I had known.

They screamed. But not Karen. She looked at me with a look of terror and wonder. No, she didn't look at me. She looked through me. She saw the Lord. I was a window through which shone the light of God.

8

I came to the border. I waited in line for the guard to check my passport. I prayed that he wouldn't detain me. I eased the car into the booth, rolled down the window, and handed him the passport.

Please, God. Please.

He looked at it, at me, then typed the number into his computer. He started humming a tune I didn't recognize. After a few moments, he handed it back to me.

"Welcome to Canada, Ms. Lennox. Sweet dreams!"

I pulled through, entering the country. There was a visitor's center up ahead. I pulled into the parking lot. I put the car in park, let out a sigh, and began to cry. It felt like I had been holding my breath for days.

I looked at the passport again.

Anne Lennox.

It had worked. He was right.

I wiped my eyes and felt a sudden pang of hunger. I got back on the road and drove for a few miles, or kilometers, until I came to a Tim Horton's. I went inside, making sure to bring the gym bag with me. I ordered a chicken salad sandwich, a blueberry fritter, and a cup of coffee. Food had never tasted so good.

I found a motel. I paid in cash, having exchanged money back at the visitor's center. I went to my room, locked the door, and turned the TV on just to have some noise.

I set the gym bag on the bed. I undid the zipper and took it out.

The clear plastic cube.

What was left of her.

I had never been on my own for so long. When I had traveled, it had always been as part of Karen's entourage. Wherever we went, people knew who we were. Now I was just a young woman on a road trip, not too pretty but not too plain, either. Someone you'd notice for half a second while waiting in line.

It was exciting to be so anonymous. I felt I could do anything. But I had a task.

After I had gone to the Home Depot, I went to the bank. Karen had given me the password to a secret account she maintained. I withdrew the entire account, putting the money in a pouch I tucked into the gym bag.

I had gone to the house and done what I had to do.

Then I drove to Montana, skirting the Rockies as I headed north. That was where I got the fake passport. I had found the guy online, using Carolina's laptop to set up a dummy email account. He lived in a town that was little more than a stoplight. But his house was like a command center, filled with computers, machinery, and ammunition.

Making fake IDs with the names of musicians was his trademark. It actually made you safer, he told me. If people recognize your name and connect it to something familiar, they're far less likely to suspect you of anything.

That was good to know. But who was Anne Lennox?

He just laughed.

The fake passport was pretty routine. But my next request was much more unusual. If he thought it was bizarre, however, he didn't show it. Probably wasn't even the strangest request he'd ever heard. I'll bet it was up there, though.

He had put me in touch with a local artist, one who specialized in working with unusual materials. The artist wasn't shocked, either. In fact, he was enthusiastic about the project, in a way that I found off-putting, honestly. He went on about rituals and acts of remembrance, using a bunch of words I hadn't recognized. There was one thing, however, that made me sure he was right for the job. Not that I had much choice.

"The bones of the saints," he said. "Fingernails, hair clippings.

Worshipers would place them on an altar at the cathedral and pray to them for healing."

"I guess she was a saint," I said.

"Come back tomorrow."

First thing in the morning, I went to the artist's studio. He showed me a table in his workroom. There was an object on it, a white cloth draped over it. He took the edge of the cloth and tugged it off.

"Behold," he said.

There was Karen's foot, encased in a cube of Lucite. It caught the light like a prism.

I approached. I held out my hand and grazed the cube with my fingertips. I thought I felt it vibrating, though it appeared perfectly still.

I thanked the artist and paid him. He asked me what I was going to use it for.

"To tell a story," I said.

And now it was sitting on the bed of my motel room.

I couldn't stay here long. Nancy would have sent Steve out to find me. They'd think I had defaced Karen's body, blasphemed it, when the exact opposite was the case. But I didn't expect them to believe that. They thought they owned her, and wouldn't stop until they had reclaimed their property.

I had to keep moving. I needed help. And I knew just where to find it.

9

Over the next five days, I drove nearly the entire length of Canada, heading east on the Queen Elizabeth Highway. I stopped whenever I saw a Tim Horton's, recreating my first meal there to see how it held up. It was always just as good.

I stayed in local motels, avoiding the chains. I put quarters in the Magic Fingers and closed my eyes as the bed vibrated. I was barely speaking, the only conversations I had were with cashiers and clerks, and my vow of silence allowed my mind to consider all that had happened to me.

Karen had told me she'd had it backwards. Her foot wasn't possessed or under threat. That was Steve's idea, he'd been the one who had put it in her head. No, her foot had been chosen by God to perform a task greater than any she could accomplish on her own. The part is greater than the whole.

But what was the task? She couldn't say. God had chosen not to reveal that information to her. But she believed that I was the one to discover what it was.

Did I believe I was the one? Not on my own. I never would have been able to believe such a thing about myself. But I believe Karen, and she believed in me.

Karen had been slightly mistaken, however. I couldn't do this on my own. That was why I was going to find Carolina.

I crossed the border at Niagara Falls. The tasteful displays and museums were on the Canadian side, the garish souvenir shops and tourist traps on the American. I drove through upstate New York, feeling wary now that I was back in the country. I couldn't help but keep checking the rearview mirror to see if I was being followed. Steve may have been having the same thoughts as me, but I still had to risk it. It was the only way.

I took the Lincoln Tunnel and started crawling through Manhattan. I felt homesick. Not for anything I had experienced, but for what I had imagined. Me and Carolina, trying to make it in the big city. Splitting the rent on an overpriced closet, eating ramen every night. Taking this road trip by myself, something I thought I'd never do, was making me think about other possibilities I could have pursued. The good career, the bad boyfriend. I would never have any of it.

But I did have something. This task I'd been given was more than I would have expected for myself. It was extraordinary, even though I was still an ordinary young woman. It gave me the confidence to see my task to the end without getting distracted by missed opportunities.

I crossed the bridge into Brooklyn. It took me almost an hour to find a parking spot. I got the gym bag from the trunk, slung it over my shoulder, and began walking. Did I look like I belonged here? Would the skinny girls with black plastic glasses think I was a fraud?

I hurried, not wanting to be late. It was Sunday, and Mass was starting at St. Gregory's.

The cathedral was a beautiful old building. We didn't have churches like this in Colorado. I entered and soon grew distracted by the gorgeous stained glass windows depicting scenes from the lives of the saints, catching the sunlight, folding it, shaping it, like origami.

What would Karen look like, rendered in stained glass?

What would I look like?

I found her sitting in the back corner, the only one in the pew. She was praying along with the liturgy, head bowed, chin tucked. The priest finished his prayer and she looked up to find me sitting next to her.

"It came true," she said.

"What did?"

"My prayer. I prayed that you would come."

"You said you didn't believe."

"I've been considering the possibility."

We left the sanctuary and found a small prayer chapel in the back corner of the building. There was a small altar on one side, a crucifix on the wall behind it.

She asked where I had been. I told her where I had traveled. I didn't mention the artist or the commission I'd given him, however.

"What about you? What happened?" I said.

"Nancy was furious, of course. Steve accused me of influencing you, goading you to do it to make for a better story. 'The secular media cares only for its own glorification,' he said. They called the police and a detective actually tried to confiscate my materials, my laptop, and all my notes, but I refused. Breach of journalistic integrity. Nancy tried to have me arrested, but the legal department from Browsr called the police and told them in no uncertain terms what my rights were."

"You had to've been so strong to go through that. I know how Nancy can get."

"What about how you can get? What happened to you?"

"I don't know if I can explain it. It's okay if you don't understand."

"I want to understand."

She reached over and placed her hand on mine. Before, a gesture of friendship like this would have made me leap for joy. But now, I couldn't help but wonder if there was something behind it.

"Are you still writing your story?"

"My editor still wants it. She thinks I can change it from a profile to a first-person feature. One reporter's harrowing story."

"That sounds good for you."

"But is it good for you? Is your story over, or are we still in the middle of it?"

She sensed that something more needed to be done. Would she help me discover the task Karen had sent me to find?

That reminded me. "What happened to Karen?"

"What happened? She's dead, that's what happened."

Karen had told me that she wasn't going to live, but I hadn't been able to fully believe it. I began crying in the chapel. Carolina apologized for being sharp, but I told her it was okay.

"She asked you to do it, right?" Carolina said.

"She said I was the only one who could do it."

"Was it assisted suicide? Some sort of unorthodox euthanasia?"

"No, Karen didn't want to end her life. She never would have done that."

"But she did, in fact. She got you to do it."

"Her dying was just a side effect. There was something important we had to do."

"And what was that?"

I unzipped the gym bag.

She leapt up and recoiled against the wall. I was disappointed, honestly. Being Catholic, going to Mass, I thought she would understand the devotion of it. The bones of the saints and all that. But she thought I was crazy, same as anyone else would have done.

"She told you to do this?" she said.

"No, I found someone to encase it like this, make it last."

"But she still told you to cut it off and carry it around like a lock of hair?"

"It's what it was meant for. That's what she finally understood, what other people couldn't see. Her work was done. But her foot wasn't. There's something more it needs to do."

"Get displayed on a mantelpiece?" Carolina said. Was this what Catholics did, make jokes about what was most serious?

"I thought you would understand. You wrote all those articles about the Virgen, icons and symbols of devotion. Isn't this what we're supposed to do?"

She looked at me, at the foot, then at the door. Did she think I was insane, that I was going to hurt her? Quite possibly. But she would have thought of something else: this would make a great story, the subject coming to the reporter and asking her to be a part of it. This could be even better than she had imagined.

I didn't begrudge her these thoughts. If anyone was going to tell this story, I wanted it to be her.

"So you think there's something we need to do with this," she said.

"I know there is. I just don't know what. I came here because I thought you might. Do you?"

She looked at the foot, steeling herself not to flinch.

"We should take her home," she said.

"We can't go back to Colorado."

"Not that home."

I saw what she meant. Ohio. Nancy's house, where the accident had happened.

It was perfect, just what we needed to do. I should have been able to think of it on my own. But if I had, I wouldn't have come here for Carolina. And she needed to be part of the story.

We had to hurry. We went to my car. Two young women on a cross-country road trip! Singing along to the radio, stopping at gas stations for junk food. It might have been disrespectful to think of our spiritual pilgrimage like this, but I couldn't help myself.

I buckled my seatbelt and put the key in the ignition. I checked the rearview mirror.

And I saw him.

"There are many parts, but one body," Steve said.

10

The first thing he did was take our phones. My flip phone, Carolina's smart phone. He snapped mine in half like he was breaking a twig, then used both hands to break Carolina's down the middle like he was splitting up a chocolate bar. He tossed them out the window and told me to drive.

"Where am I headed?" I asked him, trying to be polite about it.

"Same place you were headed before."

He had been expecting me to return to the house. Nancy was there right now, in fact, in case I had shown up before Steve could track me down. But now we could all meet together.

Steve had arrived in Brooklyn two days ago. He had been keeping an eye on Carolina the whole time, seeing if I would make contact with her, or vice versa. I was angry with myself for being so predictable. I had put Carolina in greater danger than she had ever asked for, and I might very well have blown my chance to accomplish my task.

Unless this was somehow part of it? Were we meant to face this challenge? I couldn't know, so I had to trust. Would Carolina do the same?

Just before we got on the bridge, Steve told me to pull over. I found a gas station and pulled into the parking lot.

"You're free to go," he said.

I turned my head. He told me to turn back around, keep my eyes on the road.

"Doesn't Nancy want to see me?"

"Not you. Her."

Carolina looked at me. There was fear in her eyes, even more than I had seen when we were in Karen's bedroom. She wanted to leave. I didn't know if I could do this without her. It was selfish to want her to stay with me, maybe even sinful, but I couldn't help it.

"He wants you to," I said. "He wants you to leave me alone."

"Carolina was just about to leave," said Steve.

She unbuckled her seatbelt.

I hated Steve for making me twist her emotions like this. I was doing just what he wanted me to do, putting her in danger, then having me make her feel guilty about it. This was what he had done to Karen, and now he was doing it to me.

"You'll need someone to read the map, now that we don't have our phones," she said, putting her seatbelt back on.

"So be it," said Steve. "That was the only mercy you'll be shown. Don't ask for it again."

I turned the car back on. We crossed the bridge, got on the highway, and left the city.

Being held hostage will make you appreciate the ordinary moments of beauty that you might miss in less stressful circumstances.

Truck stops and fast food restaurants had never looked so appealing. Every sign we passed was like the window of a charming little home, through which you could see a nice family living their lives in peace and calm. Billboards for double bacon cheeseburgers were like offerings of sanctuary.

I asked Steve if we could stop somewhere, get something to eat.

"We have a schedule to keep," he said.

"What schedule? Karen isn't going to get any more dead, is she?"

Even Carolina was shocked at how brazen I was.

He let me take the next exit. Signs for food, gas, and lodging along the side of the road. There was one for exactly what I wanted: Steak 'n Shake.

When I was younger and we still lived in Ohio, Nancy used to take me there. Just the two of us. A chocolate milkshake for her, a junior vanilla for me. I wanted to go there one last time.

I parked the car, got out, and went to the trunk. Steve asked me what I was doing. I told him I had to keep something safe.

I took out the gym bag and brought it into the restaurant with me.

I hadn't been to a Steak 'n Shake in years. We didn't have them in Colorado. The black, red, and white tiles made me feel like a child again, which was appropriate. Jesus said we should have the faith of a little child, and what else was I doing but being faithful?

Steve directed us to a booth. He had Carolina and I sit on one side while he sat on the other.

I didn't even need to look at the menu. I ordered the same meal I did when I was a kid: single steakburger with cheese, hold the onion, fries, and a vanilla milkshake. I ordered the full-size rather than the junior, however.

Carolina ordered the same, though she chose a strawberry milkshake instead of vanilla. Steve ordered a bowl of chili and coffee.

"Nancy used to bring you here," he said.

"A cherished memory. One of the few I have."

"She always took care of you. She still is, even if you refuse to see it. Satan has you in his clutches, same as he did Karen."

"I'm doing God's work. I don't expect you to understand that."

He didn't get mad. He smiled, in fact. My behavior was just what he would have expected from one of Satan's agents.

"Have you considered that neither God nor Satan is behind all of this?" said Carolina. "Maybe Karen did what she did because it was the story she wanted to tell."

"You think you don't believe in anything, but the human heart always believes," said Steve. "It is its nature. I tell you it is better to believe in the Devil and know it than it is to delude yourself into thinking you hold no beliefs."

"Does that mean I'm the better servant?" I said.

"You have zeal, even if it is misdirected. Though I don't think you could ever redirect it to the Lord. You are too full of selfishness, thinking you deserve to have more than you do."

"I am nothing if not selfless. That was how I was able to do what I did."

"You were able to do what you did because the devil steadied your hand."

Some of the other customers were starting to glance over at our table. Having their attention gave me an idea.

I had placed the gym bag under the table. Now I reached down and unzipped it, took out the Lucite cube and placed it on the table, right next to my milkshake.

It was part of Steve's job to never flinch or get shaken up. But when he saw the foot, he couldn't help but recoil, grabbing the table with his hands and pushing himself back into the red pleather seat.

The other customers were now openly looking at us. I welcomed the attention. I wanted people to see it.

A teenage girl sharing a milkshake with her first boyfriend took out her phone and pointed it at us. She tapped the screen and took a photo. She would post it online, the picture getting shared on Facebook, retweeted on Twitter, liked on Instagram. I envisioned it spreading across the internet, an object at once revolting and fascinating. It would become a digital icon, the founding relic of a new faith. Karen's story would get told and re-told, acquiring new meanings, inspiring new forms of devotion.

Steve grabbed it off the table and shoved it back into the gym bag. He got out of the booth, shouldered the bag, and made us follow him. I hadn't even finished my milkshake. He flung two twenties at the cash register and left without getting change.

We got back on the road, Steve reprimanding me for my carelessness.

"I'd ask you what you thought you were doing back there, but I know the answer. It was the devil in you, making a scene for your own amusement."

"I was telling Karen's story, spreading her message. Like the roses in Juan Diego's cloak."

"Catholic idolatry? Did she give you that idea?"

"It's not idolatrous," said Carolina. "It's a beautiful story."

"A beautiful story you don't believe in."

"You have no idea what I do or do not believe."

"So tell us," Steve said.

So she did.

Her parents were Chilean. Her father worked for the military as a Navy captain, her mother stayed home and raised the children. When her father was working his way up the chain of command, the person in charge of the country was also from the military. General Pinochet. A dictator who killed thousands of people, though her father never would have used those terms. He loved Pinochet, and credited him for his own success.

Life in Chile was all connected. The military, the family, the church: all parts of the same whole. The priest of the parish that Carolina's family belonged to would offer up a blessing to the General during the liturgy. But life was changing.

When her mother was pregnant with Carolina, her fourth child, General Pinochet made an announcement. He was stepping down as dictator. Chile was going to become a democracy. Many people were thrilled with the news, looking forward to this new day for their country. Carolina's family, however, was devastated. For them, Pinochet was Chile. If he was leaving, so would they.

Her father had connections with the US military, and they got him a position as a consultant. They moved to Washington, DC, when her mother was eight months pregnant. Before they were even finished unpacking, Carolina was born. An American citizen.

Her family found a Catholic parish that shared their conservative beliefs. Carolina grew up in the faith, mostly bored by the liturgies and her parents' evocations of lost Chilean glory. When she went off to college, however, she quickly embarrassed herself by speaking matter-of-factly about Pinochet. He was a mythic

60

figure her father droned on about during Sunday dinner. But her friends were shocked. Pinochet was a monster, they told her. She did her homework to see if they were right. They were.

She was furious. At her family, at her country, at her church. Over Thanksgiving break, she declared to her parents that she was now an atheistic communist. Her father cursed her for being an ungrateful, spoiled American girl. She ran to her bedroom and slammed the door. She texted her friends and told them what had happened. They applauded her with exclamation points and emoticons, hearts and smiley faces.

College became one long argument, Carolina and her friends on one side, the whole world on the other. Included in the world was Catholicism. She gathered instances of its failures like she was taking a census. Anyone who tried to defend the church on the basis of the support it provided to the lower classes was dismissed immediately.

What made her soften her position, however, was not another argument. It was a story.

One of her friends was the daughter of Mexican immigrants, itinerant construction workers whose American dream was realized when their daughter won a scholarship to an elite East Coast university. She had grown up hearing the story of the Virgen de Guadalupe, had even visited the shrine in Mexico City, and she was the one to tell it to Carolina, waiting politely until she was finished with one of her tirades. Carolina was familiar with the image of the Virgen, of course, and had heard many elements of the story before, but hearing it from her friend gave her the sense she was hearing a creation myth for the first time, its strangeness and beauty suddenly apparent.

What made religion unique were not the rules or hierarchies. It was the stories. And what made the stories was the fact that they were continuously getting retold, communities emphasizing one aspect of a story while ignoring others in order to tell the story they needed to tell.

The story of the Virgen insisting on having her message heard was the story Carolina needed to hear. It showed how the best of what the Church was could be greater than its worst. The story would always break through.

That was her answer to Steve's question. What did she believe? She believed in the Virgen. She believed that a silly little listicle meant to accrue shares and likes could still communicate the essence of the Virgen's message, that there was nowhere she would not go and nothing she would not do to tell her story.

"Idolatry, false idols," said Steve. "You are not telling a story, not the one you think. You are telling lies."

"You'll see how true it is," I said.

"You're both mistaken," said Carolina.

That brought me up short, same as Steve.

"You believe you're the ones to tell Karen's story. But you're part of it, same as her. Same as me. It's larger than all of us."

11

We arrived in Ohio later that afternoon. A medium-sized town in the middle of the state. We had moved when I was a little girl, and this was my first time back.

I forgot about the task I was here to perform, getting caught up with seeing how the town matched up with the memories I had of it. I recognized a distinctively colored slide in a public park, though the paint was faded, like an item of clothing that had been washed numerous times. There was the church we used to attend, the school where I went to kindergarten. It was as if someone had looked into my memories and constructed an entire town based on what little I could recall of my childhood.

Steve directed me to the house. It was a good thing he was here, actually. I wouldn't have been able to remember where it was.

A two-story home in the town's nicest neighborhood. I had forgotten that Nancy's parents were well-off. Her father had been a vice president at a regional company based in town. The house was one of those McMansions, constructed when they were first becoming popular: three bedrooms, an open basement for a play area, a spacious deck, and a swimming pool.

After the divorce, Nancy had bought the house from her parents with Karen's money. There had been discussions of turning it into a museum, where Karen's fans could come and hear her story in the very place where it had started, but Nancy had never taken the initiative to make it happen. It was the one plan she had never carried out.

Steve had me park in the driveway. He waited for me and Carolina to get out, then escorted us inside.

If the town was based on my memories, then the house was a memory itself. Stepping through the doorway felt like stepping into my own head. I recognized the rooms, but at a physical level more than a mental one. My body could recall running through these rooms when I was a little girl. There was an ache in my muscles I couldn't quite place, like the unscratchable itch of a phantom limb.

The furniture was covered in plastic, like meat placed in the freezer to keep from spoiling. Pictures had been taken off the walls and stacked against the baseboards like decks of cards.

"You grew up here," Carolina said.

"We lived with my grandparents for the first few years, before Karen's ministry really took off. Nancy didn't have the money for a place of her own."

"Your grandparents must have liked having you around."

"They were always uncomfortable, like they were the guests instead of me and Nancy."

Steve kept us moving until we came to the kitchen. There were windows that let in the night, illuminating the dust motes in the air. I felt like we were floating in space, surrounded by the debris of a ruptured moon.

Next to the refrigerator stood Nancy.

"Welcome home," she said.

"It hasn't been home for a long time," I said.

"We did make a home for ourselves, and a family to go with it, but you've destroyed them both."

"I didn't destroy anything you hadn't already broken."

"You think you know what's broken? You know nothing. You wouldn't be able to take it. That's why I protected you from it for so long."

"I can protect myself now."

"Can you protect her?" Nancy nodded at Carolina. "The best friend you've always wanted. What will you do when she's done playing?"

"I can take care of myself," said Carolina.

"But can you take care of Hannah? That's what she wants you to do, you know."

"I'm here to see what happens so I can tell her story."

"That's good. She'd never be able to tell it on her own. I've come to think that was Karen's real reason for bringing you out to do your story. She wanted to give Hannah someone to talk to."

I know she said that to try to hurt me, but it simply made me even more grateful for all that Karen had done for me. Nancy would have to try harder if she really wanted to cause me pain.

She tried harder.

"Steve said you brought me a gift."

He took the gym bag from my hand and placed it on the island in the center of the kitchen. He zipped it open and stepped back.

I reached inside and took it out.

Nancy wasn't shocked like everyone else had been. She looked vindicated, if anything, as if things were turning out exactly as she expected.

Nancy said to Carolina, "Did she get this idea from you? One of your listicles about Shroud of Turin beach towels?"

"It was all her," Carolina said with something like admiration in her voice. Did she now think I was right, or did she still think I was crazy? Maybe she thought I had gone crazy for the right reason.

That was fine by me.

"I know you've had your fun, taking this road trip of yours, but it's time for you to give me that. I can still salvage something of her legacy, no matter what lies Browsr tells."

She waited for me to bring it to her.

Steve took a step closer. He was inches away from me. The hairs on my neck stood up from his proximity.

I looked at Carolina. There was sympathy in her eyes, even understanding. But would she understand what I was about to do?

I gripped the Lucite cube tight, wound up like an athlete throwing a shot put and smashed it into the front of Steve's head.

The artist had constructed it well; it didn't even crack. Steve's left eye oozed out of its socket like a melting candle.

He collapsed to the floor. Nancy shouted. Now she was surprised.

I tucked the cube under my arm and ran out of the kitchen. I ran downstairs to the rec room. There was the pool table, covered in vinyl. I dashed past it to the back door. I forced it open and stumbled out into the sunlight.

There it lay before me.

The swimming pool.

It was empty. It yawned like a canyon. I walked to the nearest edge. I took my shoes off, putting the toes of one foot to the heel of the other. I kicked them down into the pool. They clattered like stones on the tile.

I walked around to the diving board. I stepped onto it, the soles of my feet gripping the pebbly surface. I inched forward until I was at the very edge.

Nancy came out of the door, followed closely by Carolina. They looked far away, as if they were on the opposite shore of a vast lake. But I could still make out the look of concern on Carolina's face.

She didn't understand, not right now. But she would.

I began bouncing the board with my feet, holding the cube steady at my chest.

"Do it," said Nancy.

I was going to.

"Be just like her."

I could never be just like Karen, but I could aspire.

"You are her sister, after all."

12

Nancy sat on the diving board, praying to God, asking him to heal Karen. If he could take the suffering in Karen's body and place it in hers, she would gladly bear the burden. She prayed, and prayed, and prayed.

In the hospital, Karen felt the first twinge of sensation in her foot. But Nancy didn't know that. She thought God had forsaken her. She looked up at the heavens and cursed his name. She no longer believed He was good. A God who was good, who cared for His children, wouldn't have let this happen.

She stood up from the diving board. She saw a figure standing in the doorway.

Les.

He had heard her curse God. She mustn't do that, she needed to keep her faith. For her transgression, she needed to be punished.

The Lord rebukes those that he loves most.

Les stepped onto the deck. Nancy tried to run, but the diving board was too wobbly. By the time she made it off, Les was standing before her.

He grabbed her wrist. She tried to twist free, but he was too strong. He grabbed her other wrist and held both her hands before her face. She stared at them wide-eyed, like a saint beholding her own stigmata.

He led her inside. He dragged her up the stairs, to her own bedroom.

The whole time, Nancy prayed that she wouldn't remember this, that God would remove it from her memory. He didn't.

Nancy was still on the opposite side of the pool, but Carolina had begun walking around the edge to the diving board.

Carolina was talking to me. I could hear her, finally.

"You don't have to do this, it's not who you are."

How could I not do this? How could I be anyone else?

"Your story doesn't have to end this way."

There is only one way a story can end.

"I'm not saying this because you're the subject of my story. I'm saying this because you're my friend."

I had a friend. And a sister. This was quite the day. But I couldn't do what Carolina asked. My choice had been made before I was even born.

I looked at my mother. I held my half-sister, the fraction of her that was left. I straightened my back, arched my toes and gave the diving board a bounce.

And the Lord carried me, his precious child.

Colophon

Cover and titles are in Modern No. 20.
Body font is in Constantia.

About the Author

Adam Fleming Petty was born in Chicago, raised in Indiana, and educated in Michigan. He now lives in Indianapolis with his wife and two daughters. His writing has appeared in *Electric Literature*, the *Paris Review Daily*, the *Los Angeles Review of Books*, and *The Millions*. He is at work on a novel about Dungeons & Dragons in Iraq.

Etchings Press

Etchings Press is a student-run publisher at the University of Indianapolis. Each year, student editors choose the Whirling Prize, a post-publication award, in the fall and coordinate a publication contest for one poetry chapbook, one prose chapbook, and one novella in the spring. For more information, please visit etchings.uindy.edu.

Previous winners and publications

Poetry
2019: *As Lovers Always Do* by Marne Wilson
2018: *In the Herald of Improbable Misfortunes* by Robert Campbell
2017: *Uncle Harold's Maxwell House Haggadah* by Danny Caine
2016: *Some Animals* by Kelli Allen
2015: *Velocity of Slugs* by Joey Connelly
2014: *Action at a Distance* by Christopher Petruccelli

Prose
2019: *Dissenting Opinion from the Committee for the Beatitudes*
        by Marc J. Sheehan (fiction)
2018: *The Forsaken* by Chad V. Broughman (fiction)
2017: *Unravelings* by Sarah Cheshire (memoir)
2016: *Pathetic* by Shannon McLeod (essays)
2015: *Ologies* by Chelsea Biondolillo (essays)
2014: *Static: Stories* by Frederick Pelzer (fiction)

Novella
2019: *Savonne, Not Vonny* by Robin Lee Lovelace
2018: *Edge of the Known Bus Line* by James R. Gapinski
2017: *The Denialist's Almanac of American Plague and Pestilence*
        by Christopher Mohar
2016: *Followers* by Adam Fleming Petty

www.ingramcontent.com/pod-product-compliance
Lightning Source LLC
Chambersburg PA
CBHW070317120726
47910CB00007B/2516